THE HERALDS OF LIGHT

THERE'S ALWAYS HOPE EMBEDDED IN THE DARK,
ALL YOU NEED IS A LITTLE DIGGIN' UP TO FIND IT

AKAANSHA SENGUPTTA

Made with ♥ on the Notion Press Platform
www.notionpress.com

Contents

CHAPTER ONE

In a world that was once ruled by magic and mysticism, a great upheaval had taken place. A powerful force known as the "Divine Empress" had risen to power, wielding her incredible abilities to control and manipulate the very fabric of reality. Her rule was absolute, and none dared to challenge her, for fear of her wrath.

However, in the midst of this darkness, there emerged a group of individuals known as the "Heralds of Light." These brave men and women were gifted with the power to manipulate light and had vowed to overthrow the Empress and restore balance to the world.

One such Herald was a young girl named Akira, who had been born with the ability to control the very essence of light itself. From a young age, she had trained tirelessly under the guidance of her master, the wise and powerful "Lightbringer."

Under the Lightbringer's tutelage, Akira had become one of the most skilled and powerful Heralds in the land, and she had dedicated herself to the cause of the Heralds, fighting to overthrow the Empress and bring about a new age of peace and prosperity.

However, Akira's path was not an easy one, for the Empress had spies and agents everywhere, seeking to eliminate the Heralds at every turn. Akira found herself constantly on the run, fighting for her life and the lives of her fellow Heralds.

In the midst of her struggles, Akira met a young man named Kaito, who had also dedicated himself to the cause of the Heralds. Kaito was a talented fighter, but he lacked the finesse and control that Akira possessed.

Despite their differences, Akira and Kaito formed a deep bond, and they became inseparable partners in the fight against the Empress. Together, they traveled the land, battling the Empress's minions and rallying the people to their cause.

As their quest continued, Akira and Kaito encountered a host of other Heralds, each with their own unique abilities and stories. They fought alongside powerful mages, swift warriors, and even a group of rogue scientists who had dedicated themselves to using their intellect and technology to combat the Empress.

But as the Heralds' ranks grew, so too did the Empress's power. Her armies of darkness seemed unstoppable, and her grip on the land grew ever tighter.

In a final desperate battle, Akira and her fellow Heralds confronted the Empress in her throne room. The battle was fierce, and the Empress's power seemed nearly insurmountable. But with the help of Kaito and the other Heralds, Akira was able to summon a final burst of energy, unleashing the full extent of her light-manipulating powers.

In a blinding flash of light, the Empress was defeated, her powers broken, and the world was plunged into a new era of peace and freedom.

As the people rejoiced, Akira and Kaito stood together, watching as the sun rose on a new day. Though their struggles had been long and difficult, they knew that the battle had been worth it, for they had ushered in a new age of hope and promise, where the light of freedom would always shine bright.

CHAPTER TWO

In the aftermath of the battle, Akira and the other Heralds were hailed as heroes. The people of the land held grand celebrations in their honor, and many young children dreamed of growing up to become like them.

Despite the newfound peace, however, Akira knew that there was still much work to be done. The world was still recovering from the chaos of the Empress's reign, and there were still many dark corners where evil lurked.

With this in mind, Akira and Kaito set out on a new mission. They would travel the land, helping those in need and spreading the message of hope and light that they had fought so hard to defend.

Their travels took them to every corner of the world, from the bustling cities to the farthest reaches of the wilderness. They met people of all kinds, from humble farmers to powerful nobles, and they helped them in whatever way they could.

Akira's powers of light manipulation proved particularly useful in their travels. She was able to heal the sick, illuminate dark places, and even provide warmth on cold nights.

As their journey continued, Akira and Kaito's bond grew ever stronger. They faced many challenges and obstacles along the way, but they always faced them together, drawing strength from each other's presence.

It was during a particularly difficult time that Akira learned something surprising about Kaito. He revealed to her that he too possessed a special power, the ability to summon powerful winds and storms.

Together, they combined their powers to perform incredible feats, such as creating massive gusts of wind to blow away dangerous creatures or summoning lightning to strike their foes.

As they traveled, Akira and Kaito also encountered a variety of interesting characters, including a band of thieves who had taken up the cause of justice, and a group of monks who had discovered a new way of harnessing their powers.

Despite their differences, the Heralds shared a common goal - to use their powers for the greater good and to protect the world from the forces of darkness.

As they journeyed, Akira and Kaito encountered an even greater challenge. They discovered a mysterious force that threatened to plunge the world back into chaos. It was a powerful entity, known only as "The Darkness," and it seemed to feed on the fears and negative emotions of the people.

Akira and Kaito knew that they had to act quickly to stop The Darkness from spreading. They rallied their fellow Heralds and set out to confront it.

The battle was long and grueling, but the Heralds never gave up. In the end, they were able to drive The Darkness back, using their powers of light and wind to strike at its heart.

As they stood victorious, Akira and Kaito realized that their journey was far from over. The world was still filled with challenges and dangers, but they knew that they could face them all, as long as they had each other.

And so, the two Heralds continued on their journey, their bond as strong as ever. Together, they continued to spread the message of hope and light, always ready to stand against whatever forces might threaten the peace and freedom that they had fought so hard to achieve.

CHAPTER THREE

Several years had passed since Akira and Kaito's victory over The Darkness. The world had been at peace, and the Heralds had become beloved figures throughout the land. But one day, a young woman arrived in their midst, claiming to be the long-lost daughter of the Empress, thought to have been lost during the war.

Akira and Kaito were skeptical at first, but as they listened to her story, they began to believe that she might indeed be who she claimed to be. The young woman's name was Hikari, and she bore an uncanny resemblance to the Empress. She also possessed a unique power - the ability to control shadows.

Despite their misgivings, Akira and Kaito agreed to help Hikari uncover the truth about her past. They set out on a quest to learn more about the young woman's origins, traveling to distant lands and seeking out ancient relics that might hold the key to her identity.

Their journey was fraught with danger, as they encountered many who sought to use Hikari's power for their own gain. They battled powerful sorcerers, dodged traps and pitfalls, and braved treacherous storms and dark forests.

As they neared the truth, they discovered that the Empress's disappearance had been orchestrated by a group of powerful mages, who had feared her growing influence and sought to remove her from power. Hikari had been taken by one of the mages, who had raised her in secret, hoping to one day use her power to overthrow the Empress's successor.

With this knowledge in hand, Akira and Kaito raced back to the capital to confront the mages and save Hikari's mother from their clutches. The mages were powerful, but the Heralds were determined to succeed. They drew upon their own powers and worked together, each bringing their unique skills to the fight.

In the end, Akira and Kaito emerged victorious. Hikari was reunited with her mother, and the mages were brought to justice. The Empress, grateful for their help, offered to make the Heralds part of her court, but they declined, preferring to continue their travels and help those in need.

As they set out once more on their journey, Akira and Kaito reflected on all that they had learned. They had faced incredible challenges and learned to trust in each other more than ever before. They had made new friends and encountered new enemies, but through it all, they had remained true to their purpose - to protect the world from the forces of darkness and to spread the message of hope and light.

And with each step they took, they knew that they were not alone. They had each other, and the world was a better place for it.

CHAPTER FOUR

Years had passed since the Heralds had last been together. Akira and Kaito had gone their separate ways, each continuing their own journey. But news of a new threat had reached them, a dark force that threatened to undo all they had accomplished.

Rumors had spread that the Empress, thought to have been defeated years before, had been reincarnated. But this time, she was not the benevolent ruler she had once been. Instead, she had been reborn as a being of pure darkness, intent on ruling the world with an iron fist.

Akira and Kaito knew that they had to act fast. They had to put aside their differences and work together once again to defeat this new threat. They set out to gather the remaining Heralds, calling upon old friends and allies to join them in their quest.

As they journeyed across the land, they encountered new dangers at every turn. The Empress's followers were everywhere, and they were determined to stop the Heralds at any cost. But the Heralds were equally determined, drawing upon their own powers and working together to overcome any obstacle.

As they approached the Empress's stronghold, they could feel the darkness growing stronger. The air was thick with it, and the sky had grown dark. But they pressed on, knowing that the fate of the world rested on their shoulders.

When they finally reached the stronghold, they were met by the Empress herself, now a twisted and corrupted version of the woman they had once known. Her power was immense, and her followers were many, but the Heralds refused to back down.

In a final battle, the Heralds faced off against the Empress and her minions, using all their power and skill to try and defeat her. It was a grueling battle, and many fell before the Heralds emerged victorious. In the end, it was Akira and Kaito who struck the final blow, banishing the Empress and her darkness back into the void.

As they surveyed the aftermath of the battle, the Heralds knew that their work was not yet done. There would always be new threats to the world, and they would need to remain vigilant to protect it. But they also knew that they could rely on each other, and that no matter what challenges lay ahead, they would face them together.

And so they parted ways once again, each setting out on their own journey. But this time, they knew that they would always be united in their mission to protect the world and spread the message of hope and light.

CHAPTER FIVE

As the Heralds went their separate ways, they knew that their adventures together had come to an end. But they also knew that their bond would never be broken, and that they would always be there for each other in times of need.

Akira returned to his hometown, where he was welcomed as a hero. He settled down and started a family, passing on the knowledge he had gained to his children and teaching them to use their own powers for good.

Kaito continued to travel, never staying in one place for too long. He wandered the world, seeking out new adventures and helping those in need. His name became known far and wide, and he was remembered as a legend in his own time.

As for Hikari, she returned to the capital, where she was welcomed back as the rightful heir to the throne. She ruled with wisdom and compassion, determined to make the world a better place for all its inhabitants. She also remained in contact with Akira and Kaito, sending them messages and updates on the state of the world.

Years passed, and the world continued to change. New threats emerged, but the Heralds were always there to face them. They passed their knowledge on to new generations of heroes, ensuring that the legacy of their adventures would never be forgotten.

In the end, the Heralds were remembered not only as powerful warriors, but as symbols of hope and light in a dark and uncertain world. Their story became legend, inspiring future generations to stand up against darkness and fight for what was right.

And even though they had gone their separate ways, the Heralds always remembered the bond that had brought them together. They remained lifelong friends, united by their shared experiences and the knowledge that they had made a difference in the world.

CHAPTER SIX

It had been centuries since the Heralds of Light had passed into legend. The world had changed, and the stories of their adventures had become nothing more than myths and legends. But the forces of darkness that the Heralds had once fought against had not been defeated. They had only been lying in wait, biding their time until the world was once again ripe for conquest.

In the year 2033, the world was a very different place. Technology had advanced to a level that the Heralds could never have imagined, and the world was connected in ways that had once seemed impossible. But despite all the progress, there was a darkness that had settled over the world. People had become disconnected from each other, and the forces of greed and power had taken over.

It was in this world that Akira's great-great-great-great-great-great-great-great-great-great-great-great-great-granddaughter, Aya, was born. Like her ancestor, Aya possessed a great power, the ability to create. But unlike the Heralds of Light, Aya had never been trained in the use of her powers. She was unaware of the great legacy of her family, and knew nothing of the darkness that threatened the world.

It wasn't until a chance encounter with a group of rebels that Aya learned of her family's legacy. The rebels had been fighting against the forces of darkness, and they knew that

Aya was the only one who could turn the tide of the battle. They convinced her to join them, and together they set out to fight against the darkness that threatened the world.

At first, Aya was hesitant. She had never used her powers before, and she was unsure of her abilities. But as she fought alongside the rebels, she began to understand the true power of her gifts. With each use of her powers, she grew stronger, more confident, and more in control of her abilities.

Together, Aya and the rebels faced off against the forces of darkness, using their combined powers to push back against the darkness that had threatened to engulf the world. They fought tirelessly, never giving up, and never losing sight of their goal. And in the end, they emerged victorious, banishing the darkness back to where it came from.

As Aya looked out over the world she had helped to save, she knew that the legacy of her family would never be forgotten. The stories of the Heralds of Light may have faded into myth, but the spirit of hope and courage that they had embodied still lived on. And with her own newfound strength and her connection to her family's legacy, Aya knew that she would always be ready to fight against the darkness, no matter where it may arise.

CHAPTER SEVEN

After the victory over darkness, Aya returned to her normal life. She enrolled in a prestigious high school, hoping to have a normal teenage experience. She had always been homeschooled, so this was a new and exciting chapter in her life. However, Aya soon realized that being a hero in the eyes of the world didn't guarantee popularity or acceptance in school.

Aya was always different from her classmates. She had powers that no one else had, and her unique upbringing made her stand out. She was constantly being watched and scrutinized by her peers, who were curious about her but also scared of her abilities. Despite her best efforts to fit in, Aya felt like an outsider, and she longed for the acceptance that seemed to come so easily to others.

She tried to keep her powers a secret, not wanting to draw attention to herself. However, her attempts were futile, and it wasn't long before rumors started to spread. Aya became the subject of gossip, with some claiming that she was a witch, while others said she was an alien. Aya felt like she was being ridiculed and ostracized, and she found it hard to find her place in this new world.

Aya's only solace was her friendship with a few fellow outcasts. They were a group of misfits who didn't fit into the social hierarchy of the school. They accepted Aya for who she was and didn't judge her for her powers. They were her true friends, and Aya cherished their bond.

As the years passed, Aya started to gain more control over her powers. She became more confident and began to embrace her differences. She even started using her powers to help others, which brought her a sense of fulfillment that she had never experienced before.

Aya's confidence and positive attitude soon began to attract attention. Her classmates started to see her in a different light, and some even began to befriend her. Aya realized that being true to herself was the key to being accepted, and that she didn't need to hide her powers to fit in.

In the end, Aya learned that being a hero didn't mean being perfect or having all the answers. It was about using her unique gifts to make a difference in the world. She discovered that true acceptance and popularity come from being yourself and not trying to conform to the expectations of others.

As Aya graduated from high school, she realized that her journey wasn't over. She still had a duty to use her powers to help others, and she knew that she would continue to fight against the darkness that threatened the world. But she also knew that she had friends who would always be by her side, and that no matter what challenges lay ahead, she was ready to face them head-on.

CHAPTER EIGHT

Years went by, and Aya continued to use her powers to help those in need. She became a renowned hero in her own right, with people around the world looking up to her as a symbol of hope and strength.

However, as time passed, Aya began to notice a disturbing trend. The world seemed to be sliding back into darkness, with evil and despair creeping back into people's hearts. Aya knew that she couldn't fight this darkness alone, and she decided to look for others who shared her vision of a better world.

Aya traveled the world, seeking out those who had the potential to be heroes. She found people from all walks of life, each with their own unique abilities and strengths. Some were hesitant to join her cause, while others were eager to be part of something greater than themselves.

Aya knew that she needed a plan to unite these heroes and to fight the darkness that threatened the world. She called her team the "Guardians of Light," and she began to train them to use their abilities to protect the world.

The Guardians of Light quickly became a force to be reckoned with. They traveled the world, fighting evil wherever it appeared. They were respected and admired by people everywhere, and their heroics inspired a new generation of heroes to rise up and fight for what was right.

Aya knew that the Guardians of Light would need to be ready for anything, and she continued to train them relentlessly. They honed their abilities, both individually and as a team, and they learned to work together in perfect harmony. Aya knew that the key to their success was trust and teamwork, and she made sure that these were the values that guided them in everything they did.

The Guardians of Light faced many challenges over the years. They fought against the forces of darkness, battling evil creatures and powerful villains. They endured setbacks and losses, but they never gave up. They knew that they had a duty to protect the world, and they were determined to fulfill it.

As time went on, the world began to change. The darkness that had once threatened to consume everything was pushed back, and hope and light began to shine again. The Guardians of Light were hailed as heroes, and their legend spread far and wide.

In the end, Aya knew that her work was done. She had trained a new generation of heroes who were ready to take up the mantle and fight for the world. She knew that the Guardians of Light would continue to protect the world long after she was gone, and that they would be the shining beacon of hope in a dark and dangerous world.

Aya passed away peacefully, surrounded by her friends and family. She had lived a long and fulfilling life, and she knew that her legacy would live on through the Guardians of Light. She closed her eyes, content in the knowledge that the world was in good hands, and that the darkness would never triumph as long as there were heroes to fight it.

CHAPTER NINE

As the years went by, the Guardians of Light continued to face new challenges and threats.

They battled against powerful villains, dark magic, and even ancient demons that threatened to unleash chaos upon the world.

Despite the danger, the Guardians never faltered in their resolve to protect the innocent and uphold justice.

Each member of the team had their own unique strengths and abilities, and they worked together seamlessly to overcome even the toughest of foes.

As the world continued to change, the Guardians adapted and evolved, always staying one step ahead of the forces of darkness.

They became not just heroes, but symbols of hope and inspiration to people around the world.

Young people looked up to them as role models, and the Guardians took that responsibility seriously, always striving to set a positive example for others to follow.

Over the years, the team grew in number, as more and more heroes were inspired to join their cause.

Each new member brought their own unique perspective and talents, making the team stronger and more resilient than ever.

However, with the growing threats to the world, the Guardians also knew that they needed to be prepared for the worst.

They trained relentlessly, honing their skills and abilities to perfection.

They developed new technologies and weapons, always pushing the boundaries of what was possible.

And they worked closely with other heroes and organizations around the world, building a network of support and strength that could never be broken.

Despite the challenges, the Guardians of Light never lost sight of their ultimate goal: to protect the world and create a better future for all.

And as the years went by, that goal became closer and closer to reality.

The forces of darkness were pushed back, and the world began to heal from the wounds of the past.

The Guardians knew that they couldn't take all the credit for this progress, but they were proud of the part they had played in it.

They continued to work tirelessly, always vigilant for any new threats that might emerge.

And even when they faced setbacks or losses, they never gave up.

They knew that the fight for justice and peace was never truly over, and that they would always be needed to protect the world.

Over time, the members of the team grew older and passed the mantle to the next generation of heroes.

But the legacy of the Guardians of Light lived on, inspiring new heroes to rise up and fight for what was right.

And as the world entered a new era of peace and prosperity, the Guardians of Light looked back on their long and storied history with pride.

They knew that they had made a difference in the world, and that their legacy would live on for generations to come.

The team members continued to keep in touch, sharing stories of their adventures and reminiscing about the battles they had fought together.

They knew that their bond would never be broken, and that they would always be there for one another, no matter what.

And as they looked to the future, the Guardians of Light knew that there would be new challenges to face and new battles to fight.

But they were ready, as they had always been, and they knew that together they could overcome any obstacle that came their way.

The Guardians of Light stood as a shining example of what could be achieved when people worked together for a common cause.

And they knew that as long as there were heroes like them in the world, the forces of darkness would never be able to overcome the light.

CHAPTER TEN

Decades passed, and the world of 2033 had changed in ways that the Guardians of Light could have never imagined.

Technology had advanced beyond their wildest dreams, and the world had become more interconnected than ever before.

But even with all of these advances, there were still those who sought to use their power for evil.

The Guardians of Light had become legends, their stories passed down from generation to generation.

They were revered as heroes, and their legacy had inspired countless others to take up the cause of justice and peace.

But even with all of this, the world still needed protectors.

And so, a new generation of heroes had emerged, inspired by the stories of the Guardians of Light and eager to follow in their footsteps.

One of these new heroes was a young woman named Aria.

She had grown up hearing stories about the Guardians of Light, and she had always been inspired by their bravery and selflessness.

Aria had always known that she wanted to be a hero, and she had trained tirelessly to develop her skills and abilities.

And now, with the world facing new threats and challenges, Aria was ready to step up and do her part.

She was not alone in her quest, however.

Aria had joined forces with a team of other young heroes, each with their own unique strengths and abilities.

Together, they formed a new team of protectors, dedicated to upholding the ideals of justice and peace that the Guardians of Light had fought for so many years before.

Aria and her team faced a variety of challenges and threats.

They battled against dark magic and supernatural creatures, as well as more mundane threats such as organized crime and corrupt politicians.

But no matter what the challenge, they never wavered in their resolve.

Aria knew that being a hero was not just about fighting bad guys.

It was also about being a role model and inspiring others to do good in the world.

And so, she and her team worked closely with schools and community organizations, spreading the message of hope and optimism that the world so desperately needed.

As the years went by, Aria and her team became known as some of the greatest heroes of their time.

They were revered and respected by people all over the world, and their exploits were the stuff of legend.

But with great power came great responsibility, and Aria knew that she could never rest on her laurels.

The world was always changing, and new threats were always emerging.

And so, she and her team continued to train and hone their skills, always staying one step ahead of the forces of darkness.

In time, Aria began to realize that she was not alone in her fight.

She discovered that there were other heroes and organizations all over the world, each fighting their own battles against evil.

And so, she and her team began to reach out and forge alliances with these other heroes, creating a global network of protection and support.

Together, they were stronger than ever, and they knew that no threat could ever overcome them.

Aria's team became a force to be reckoned with, feared by those who would seek to do harm to the innocent.

They were the new guardians of light, and they were proud to carry on the legacy of the heroes who had come before them.

As time passed, Aria became a mentor to a new generation of heroes, passing on the lessons and values that she had learned throughout her long and storied career

As Aria grew older, she began to take a step back from the front lines of hero work.

Her body wasn't as strong as it once was, and she knew it was time to pass the torch to a new generation of heroes.

But even though she wasn't fighting on the front lines anymore, Aria still had a vital role to play in the world of heroism.

She became a teacher, sharing her vast knowledge and experience with young heroes who were just starting out.

Aria knew that being a hero wasn't just about fighting villains and saving the day.

It was about being a good person, someone who inspired others and made the world a better place.

And so, she taught her students not just about fighting techniques and tactics, but also about the importance of being kind, compassionate, and selfless.

Aria's students adored her, and she became a mentor to them in every sense of the word.

They looked up to her, not just as a teacher, but as a role model and a friend.

As Aria's students grew and became heroes in their own right, they carried with them the lessons that she had taught them.

They became known not just for their fighting skills, but for their kindness, their compassion, and their unwavering commitment to doing what was right.

Aria watched with pride as her students flourished, knowing that she had played a small but important part in helping to shape them into the heroes they had become.

As the years went by, Aria continued to teach and mentor young heroes.

She also remained in touch with her former teammates, who had retired from hero work and moved on to other pursuits.

They remained close, bonded by their shared experiences and their unwavering commitment to justice and peace.

Aria had lived a long and full life, but there was still one thing that she longed for.

She had always hoped to see the return of the Guardians of Light, the heroes who had inspired her to become a hero in the first place.

And then, one day, it happened.

Aria was sitting in her garden, enjoying the peace and quiet, when she heard a voice behind her.

"Hello, Aria," the voice said. "It's good to see you again."

Aria turned around, and there he was.

It was Akira, the leader of the Guardians of Light.

He looked just as she remembered him, his long white hair blowing in the breeze.

Aria couldn't believe her eyes.

"Akira," she said, her voice barely above a whisper.

"It's been so long."

Akira smiled, and Aria knew that everything was going to be okay.

They sat and talked for hours, catching up on old times and reminiscing about their adventures together.

Aria felt as though she was young again, full of hope and excitement for the future.

As they talked, Akira told Aria about his plan to bring the Guardians of Light back together.

He had been watching the world from afar, and he knew that it was time for the heroes to return.

Aria listened with rapt attention, feeling a surge of excitement building within her.

She had always believed that the world needed heroes, and she knew that the return of the Guardians of Light would be just what the world needed.

Akira explained that he had been in touch with some of their former teammates,

And that they had agreed to come out of retirement and join the cause.

Aria was overjoyed at the prospect of fighting alongside her old teammates once again.

But she also knew that there were new heroes out there, young men and women who were just as capable and just as eager to make a difference.

Akira agreed, and he and Aria set out to find and recruit the new generation of heroes.

They traveled far and wide, searching for those who had the courage, the determination, and the heart to become heroes.

And they found them.

They found young heroes who were just as dedicated to the cause as they had been in their youth.

They found heroes with incredible powers, like Aya and her ability to create and control light.

They found heroes with incredible strength, like Ryu, a young man who could lift cars with ease.

And they found heroes with incredible intelligence and ingenuity, like Kira, a young woman who could invent incredible devices that could help them fight even the toughest of foes.

Together, the old and the new heroes trained, honing their skills and learning to work as a team.

They studied the tactics and techniques that had made the Guardians of Light so successful in the past.

They learned to trust one another, to work together, and to put aside their egos and their differences for the sake of the greater good.

And then, they were ready.

The Guardians of Light emerged from the shadows, ready to face whatever challenges lay ahead.

They faced off against villains and monsters of all shapes and sizes, using their powers and their training to take down even the most formidable foes.

They fought with everything they had, never giving up or backing down in the face of danger.

And in the end, they emerged victorious.

The world cheered as the Guardians of Light emerged as the new protectors of the world.

They were a symbol of hope and strength, of justice and peace.

And they continued to inspire young heroes for generations to come.

Aria watched from afar, proud of what she had helped to create.

She had played a small but important part in bringing the Guardians of Light back to life.

And now, she knew that they would continue to inspire and protect for generations to come.

As she watched them, Aria couldn't help but think back to the day when she had first met Akira.

She had been young and inexperienced, but she had been full of hope and determination.

She had believed that she could make a difference, that she could help to make the world a better place.

And now, all these years later, she knew that she had.

She had been a hero, one of the greatest the world had ever seen.

And even though she was no longer fighting on the front lines, she knew that her legacy would live on.

Aria smiled, feeling at peace with herself and the world.

She had done what she had set out to do, and she had done it well.

And now, it was time for her to rest.

Aria closed her eyes, feeling the warmth of the sun on her face.

She breathed in the fresh air, feeling her body and mind relaxing.

She knew that she had lived a good life, one filled with adventure, excitement, and purpose.

And now, she was ready to move on to the next stage of her journey.

Aria took one last breath, feeling her body growing heavy.

She knew what was happening, but she wasn't afraid.

She had faced death many times before, and she knew that it was just another part of life.

Aria felt a sense of peace wash over her as she let go of her physical body and allowed her spirit to soar free.

She felt a sense of lightness and joy as she realized that she was no longer bound by the limitations of her mortal body.

Aria looked down and saw her body lying on the ground, but she didn't feel sad or scared.

She knew that her spirit was now free to explore new realms of existence, to discover new worlds and new adventures.

Aria felt a sense of gratitude for all of the experiences she had had in her life, both good and bad.

She knew that each experience had helped to shape her into the person she was today.

Aria looked up and saw a bright light in the distance, and she knew that it was time to move towards it.

She felt a sense of excitement and curiosity as she began to move towards the light.

As she got closer, she could see that the light was surrounded by a beautiful, golden energy.

Aria felt drawn to the energy, and she allowed it to surround her.

She felt a sense of warmth and love as the energy enveloped her, and she knew that she was home.

Aria knew that she had reached a new level of existence, one where she was surrounded by love and light.

She felt a sense of joy and wonder as she explored this new realm, discovering new sights and sounds that she had never experienced before.

Aria felt a sense of peace and contentment, knowing that she had finally found her true home.

She knew that she would always be a part of the universe, a part of the energy that flowed through all things.

Aria felt a sense of gratitude for the opportunity to live a life filled with purpose and meaning.

She knew that she had made a difference in the world, and that her legacy would live on.

Aria looked back on her life, remembering all of the adventures she had had, all of the people she had met, and all of the challenges she had overcome.

She smiled, knowing that she had lived a life that was full and rich.

Aria felt a sense of completion as she looked towards the future.

She knew that there were still many adventures to be had, both for herself and for those who came after her.

Aria felt a sense of peace and love as she realized that she was a part of something much greater than herself.

She knew that she was connected to all things, and that her spirit would live on forever.

Aria took one last look at the world she had left behind, and she felt a sense of love and gratitude for everything and everyone in it.

She knew that she had made a difference, and that her legacy would continue to inspire and guide future generations.

Aria smiled, feeling a sense of peace and contentment as she embraced her new existence, ready to continue her journey into the infinite expanse of the universe.

www.ingramcontent.com/pod-product-compliance
Lightning Source LLC
Chambersburg PA
CBHW031650170726
47990CB00019B/3107